A NORTH-SOUTH PAPERBACK

Critical praise for

Horses in the Fog

"In this sequel to *Midnight Rider*, Charlie and her friend scare themselves with a ghost story and scare the adults when they get lost in the fog. This heavily illustrated . . . easy reader features short chapters and lush watercolors, with two appealingly realistic girls and their alluring horses set against a windswept beach landscape. An especially good choice for libraries developing chapter-book fiction collections."

Booklist

Krista Ruepp

Horses in the Fog

Illustrated by Ulrike Heyne

Translated by J. Alison James

North-South Books

NEW YORK • LONDON

Copyright © 1997 by Nord-Süd Verlag AG, Gossau Zürich, Switzerland
First published in Switzerland under the title *Nebelpferde*.
English translation copyright © 1997 by North-South Books Inc.

First published in the United States, Great Britain, Canada,
Australia, and New Zealand in 1997 by North-South Books,
an imprint of Nord-Süd Verlag AG, Gossau Zürich, Switzerland.
First published in paperback in 1999.

Distributed in the United States by North-South Books Inc., New York.

Library of Congress Cataloging-in-Publication Data
Ruepp, Krista.
[Nebelpferde. English]
Horses in the fog / Krista Ruepp ; illustrated by Ulrike Heyne ;
translated by J. Alison James.
"First published in Switzerland under the title: Nebelpferde"
Summary: Charlie and her new friend Mona ride their horses out to a sand bar,
but when a sudden sea fog comes up they try to make their way back to the island,
fearing the ghost stories they've been told might be true.
[1. Islands—Fiction. 2. Fog—Fiction. 3. Horses—Fiction. 4. Ghosts—Fiction.]
I. Heyne, Ulrike, ill. II. James, J. Alison. III. Title.
PZ7. R88535Ho 1997
[Fic]—dc21 97-8736

A CIP catalogue record for this book
is available from The British Library.

ISBN 1-55858-804-3 (TRADE BINDING)
1 3 5 7 9 TB 10 8 6 4 2
ISBN 1-55858-805-1 (LIBRARY BINDING)
1 3 5 7 9 LB 10 8 6 4 2
ISBN 0-7358-1101-6 (PAPERBACK)
1 3 5 7 9 PB 10 8 6 4 2
Printed in Belgium

For more information about our books, and the authors and artists
who create them, visit our web site: http://www.northsouth.com

Contents

Old Fig's Spit Trick

It was summer on Outhorn. The small
island peacefully soaked up the midday
sun. A light wind blew and lazy waves
rustled on the sandy beach.

6

Old Fig, the local storyteller, stood in
his fishing boots, up to his hips in the
water. He was fishing for mackerel.

He watched the seagulls wheeling
above. They showed him where the fish
were. No one on the island knew the sea
as well as Old Fig did.

And no one on the island knew as many stories as he did. Especially ghost stories —Old Fig knew them all.

Old Fig spat in the water and watched intently as the little patch of foam drifted on the swell of a wave.

"Eee-yuck, Old Fig! What are you doing?" cried Charlie.

She had ridden down to the beach on Starbright and pulled up beside Old Fig.

He didn't respond.

Old Fig glared at his spittle until it dissolved.

"Why did you spit in the water?" asked Charlie.

"Because I want to catch some mackerel!" growled Old Fig.

"How does that help?" asked Charlie.

"To see if the tide has turned. Mackerel bite best when the tide's coming in."

"And how do you tell?"

"The spit goes with the tide: out to sea if the tide's going out, and in to shore if it's coming in." Old Fig grumbled, "Now look what you made me do. I didn't notice which way it was going."

Charlie jumped off the horse and spat into the water. It washed towards her. "Look!" she said. "The tide's coming in!"

"Well, it's about time," said Old Fig.

Charlie got back on the horse and galloped off, across the beach.

Charlie rode Starbright every day. Starbright was a stallion that belonged to Matthew Grimm, who lived down the road from Charlie.

It had taken a long time before Matthew Grimm allowed Charlie to go riding alone. Even now he said she had to keep to the main path or the road.

"It would be safer if you had someone to ride with," he said.

Charlie wished she could explore the whole island with Starbright, but she'd do anything to be with the stallion, so she agreed to Matthew Grimm's rules.

Mona and the Pony

Charlie rode the main path through the dunes, then between meadows and fields. The ripe yellow heads of grain bent in the summer wind. What a smell! It made Starbright frisky. Suddenly he pricked up his ears and stopped.

In the middle of a field stood a black
pony, chewing fresh oats.

A girl sat on the pony. She was kicking her heels and yanking on the reins, trying in vain to get the pony to stop eating and leave the field. Charlie thought she knew every person and every horse on the island. But she'd never seen these two.

"Hey," she called. "Do you want some help?"

"Merlin won't do anything I say," the girl said. "All he wants to do is eat."

So Charlie jumped down, tied Starbright to a fence post, and walked through the tall oats to the girl.

"Hello, I'm Charlie," she said.

"My name is Mona," said the girl. Her horse was happily munching oats. "And this is Merlin."

"He just galloped into the field with me," said Mona, "and now he won't budge."

Mona dismounted and started to pull at the reins.

Charlie pushed from behind.

But the two girls were powerless against the stubborn pony. It was a while before Merlin was finished eating. Only then would he follow the girls.

They rode together back to Mona's house.
Mona lived at the end of the island, in a
farmhouse with an old thatched roof.

"How long have you lived here?" asked
Charlie.

"We moved in last week," said Mona. "It was my grandmother's house, but we'd never even been here to visit. I didn't want to come, but my father said I could have a horse if we lived in the country. Do you want to go riding tomorrow?"

Charlie agreed to go, but she hoped Mona didn't always talk so much.

The Sandbar

The next day the two girls met by the
school. It was a hot, bright day. They rode
across the island to the beach.

As soon as they got to the sea, they led the horses into the water to cool off. Larks wheeled high in the sky, singing joyfully.

A lovely white sandbar shimmered in
the sea off the coast of Outhorn Island.
It was a nesting place for thousands of
sea birds.

"Is it shallow enough to ride over to that sand bar?" Mona asked.

"I've done it before, but never alone," said Charlie.

"You're not alone."

"Right!" Charlie laughed. "We have to be back before the tide comes in, or it will be too deep."

Starbright and Merlin set off briskly. At first the mud flats were slippery, but soon they were on firm sand. When they reached the sandbar, the girls got off and led the horses through the deep, soft sand. Terns shrieked above their heads.

"The birds build their nests in the ground here," said Charlie. "We have to watch where we're walking."

The girls plopped down in the warm sand. Through the haze they saw Outhorn far, far away. . . .

Count Brineslime

"Do you know the story of Count Brineslime?" asked Charlie.

"Who's he?" asked Mona, laughing.

"Count Brineslime is a sinister ghost who has a castle deep under the sea near Outhorn Island," said Charlie. "He kidnaps young girls and takes them to his underwater realm. They never come back."

"I don't believe it."

"It's true. Old Fig told me."

A cool wind sprang up. Then, just as suddenly, the breeze died away.

The birds were eerily silent.

Charlie jumped up.

Out across the sea she saw a wide wall
of mist, rolling right towards them.

"Sea fog," said Charlie. "Mona, get your
horse. It's time to go!"

Within minutes the bank of fog had reached the sandbar. Suddenly the girls could see nothing but white. Cold, damp air crept over their arms and legs.

The horses sucked the fog in through flared nostrils.

"We'd better ride," said Charlie. "Maybe the horses will know the right direction."

The girls mounted. Charlie could feel Starbright trembling beneath her legs. She urged him on, for she knew the tide would soon be turning.

"I hope Count Dracula doesn't get us," said Mona.

"Count Brineslime!"

"You really were joking about him, weren't you?" Mona asked.

Charlie was silent.

Horses in the Fog

Charlie rode close beside Mona. "I think we should hold hands so we don't lose each other."

Charlie took Mona's hand and squeezed it.

"I'm scared," whispered Mona.

The horses pranced nervously. Little waves washed around their hooves.

I wish I knew we were going in the right direction, thought Charlie.

Suddenly Mona screamed. "A ghost!"

Merlin stood still, rooted to the spot. He sensed Mona's fear.

"Come on. It's only the fog." Charlie urged her on. A white misty shape moved past them. It looked like it had arms, and a face that kept changing.

Charlie shivered.

Fear was creeping into Charlie along
with the cold. She kept seeing weird
things in the fog, creatures from Old Fig's
stories. Sea monsters, ghosts, and bogey
men floated up to her face and broke apart.

"Where are we?" Mona wailed.

Quick as a flash, Merlin flipped his head
back and nipped Mona's foot.

"Ow! Something bit me!" she shrieked
in a panic. She slipped and almost fell.

Charlie shook Merlin's reins firmly. "You
behave yourself," she said.

The ride across the shallows should only have taken a few minutes, but Charlie and Mona had been riding for ages now. Starbright tossed his head restlessly. It was late. He was hungry and wanted to be home.

"We should have reached Outhorn by now," said Charlie, trying to sound calm.

"We're lost," whimpered Mona. "We'll never find our way home."

What if we've ridden in a circle? thought Charlie. Or out to sea! She looked to see if the water was higher on the horses' legs. It seemed like it was.

Suddenly she remembered Old Fig's spitting trick.

"Stop a minute, Mona," cried Charlie. She jumped off her horse, knelt down and spat in the water.

Anxiously she watched the little patch of spit. She was so upset, she couldn't tell for sure. She tried again.

This time it was clear. The spit floated off to the right.

"That way!" she cried. "We have to ride that way." She pointed into the fog.

"How do you know?" asked Mona.

"The spit always moves towards shore when the tide is coming in. Old Fig showed me," Charlie said, and she got back into the saddle.

They rode steadily without talking.

Then, right ahead of them, something
dark reared up from the sea. Just as quickly
it disappeared again.

Charlie froze, her heart in her mouth.

"Count Brineslime! The sea ghost! He's coming to get us!" screamed Mona.

It took all their courage to continue on towards the dark figure.

But just then, as if they'd stepped through a door, they reached the end of the fog bank. The dark shape was right in front of them. It was the old tide marker that measured Outhorn's highest tides.

Charlie laughed in relief.

Through the haze the setting sun lit up Outhorn. Slowly the fog faded into the night sky behind them.

"We've made it!" cried Mona.

The Lights of Home

Charlie could see the lights of her house glowing across the dunes. But she had to return Starbright before she could go home. They rode up the beach at a full gallop.

The girls dismounted at the bridle path and led the horses along. Starbright whinnied and Merlin snorted. Merlin playfully nipped Starbright on his neck and snorted again. Suddenly the horses broke free and left the girls behind.

"They won't go far," said Charlie, exhausted.

The two girls walked together in silence for a while.

"You know, Charlie," said Mona. "I was really scared."

"Me too, Mona," said Charlie. "It's a good thing that we were together. It would have been scarier alone."

Mona's and Charlie's parents had been worried when they saw the sea fog roll in. Now they were out with Old Fig and Matthew Grimm, searching the dunes, the beach, and the pathways for the two riders. In the middle of the oat field they suddenly spotted two swishing tails—one black and one white.

"Over there—the horses!" shouted
Matthew Grimm.

The two horses snuffled contentedly,
chewing the delicious oats. All that riding
had made them hungry.

But where were the girls? The searchers
continued along the path. And soon the
tired girls staggered into their parents' arms.

Friends

What a reunion it was!

Happy and relieved, they all went to Mona's house.

"To celebrate the occasion, I'll donate my fresh mackerel!" said Old Fig, and he pedaled off to get it.

Mona's father took water and hay out to the horses.

Later, Charlie and Mona sat on the
sofa, wrapped in warm blankets, and
sipped hot cocoa.

"Charlie," said Mona shyly, "do you want
to go riding again with me tomorrow?"

"Sure!" said Charlie.

"We could go riding every day, if you
want," Mona said.

"Great," said Charlie. "Now I won't
have to stay on the marked paths, since
we'll be together."

When Old Fig put the grilled fish on the
table, Charlie told everyone how Old Fig's
spitting trick had saved them.

"Yes, yes, Old Fig knows a trick or two!"
he said. "Did I ever tell you the story of
the ghost ship?" And he launched into
the story.

The girls couldn't help giggling.

They weren't afraid anymore of sea ghosts or spooked ships. Nor of Count Brineslime. They'd met him today, after all. Well, sort of . . .

Krista Ruepp was born in Cologne,
Germany. After studying to be a teacher, she
worked as an editor for a German television
network, then in advertising and marketing.
Her first book for North-South, *Midnight Rider*,
introduced Charlie and the stallion Starbright.
She now lives in Remschied, Germany, with
her husband, their two sons, a dog, and an
Arabian mare.

Ulrike Heyne was born in Dresden, Germany. She studied fashion illustration and graphic design in Munich, and then spent several years working in advertising and teaching painting and drawing. She lives with her husband in Possendorf, not far from the city where she was born.

Other North-South Paperback Easy-to-Read Books